THE WINTER FLOWER

A Story of New Beginnings

For my mother,

whose courage and sacrifice paved the way for my dreams. Your journey is the heartbeat of this story. This book is for you and all the mothers who dare to dream beyond borders.

-J. Esther

To the brave souls who leave behind their homelands, sacrificing comfort and familiarity for the hope of a brighter future for their children and generations to come. Your courage and resilience inspire us all.

-Hannah

Illustrations by Hannah Otis

ISBN (Hardback) 979-8-9931192-0-5

ISBN (Paperback) 979-8-9931192-1-2

ISBN (eBook) 979-8-9931192-2-9

THE WINTER FLOWER

A Story of New Beginnings

Written by J. Esther

Illustrated by Hannah Otis

Mia looked out the window, her heart fluttering with worry about starting first grade in this strange new place. Snowy mountains stood tall in the distance, and snowflakes danced down like big, soft feathers.

She turned to her older brother, Marco. "Do you think Abuela misses us as much as we miss her?" Mia asked. "When will we see her again?"

Marco shrugged and looked away. Their mother came to sit with them on the sofa and sighed. "I don't know, Mia; it might take a while," she said gently, not wanting to worry her daughter. They had traveled a long way for a better life.

All three cuddled together, thinking of the things they missed. This mountain town felt strange and far away, with its silent streets and unfamiliar faces. Back home in Mexico, they could see the ocean sparkling in the distance, and flowers grew thick and wild on the green hillsides. Chattering parrots flew through the treetops, and the children flew kites outside the mercado, where they sold the juiciest mangoes and ice-cold coconuts.

In this new place, Mia had not yet seen children playing. Everything outside felt still, as if the world had slowed down under the frost.

Sometimes, she shivered so hard she thought her bones would break. She looked out at the gray sky, feeling a lump form in her throat. The chill bit her skin, making her feel like a tiny forgotten flower buried under layers of snow. Warm tears spilled down her cheeks.

Her mother noticed and asked gently, "Oh, Mia, *¿Qué pasa?*"

Mia met her mother's concerned gaze and, with a small, shaky voice, whispered, "I want to go back home, *Mamá*."

"Ay, Mia," her mother replied, "I know it can feel sad sometimes, but we need to be patient."

Mia turned back to the window, her heart heavy. Everything was different in the United States. The food tasted bland, strangers didn't say hello, and she only knew her mom and Marco. This place didn't feel like home, and she longed for her house in Mexico.

"Maybe breakfast will cheer you up," her mother suggested, heading to the kitchen.

She returned with a glass of freshly squeezed orange juice. Mia took a sip, and her face scrunched up. "Not even the oranges are happy here!" she exclaimed, making her mother chuckle.

The next morning, Mia's mother spent extra time braiding her hair, tying the glossy black strands with bright red ribbons. Mia grew restless, wondering if American mothers made such a fuss over their daughters' hair.

Later, on the city bus, Mia sat next to Marco as they rolled through town.
"Look! That's our new school!" Marco said, excitement in his voice.
Mia crossed her arms, feeling small and uneasy.

Inside the school, Mia's cold cheeks began to warm; a classroom full of curious faces greeted her without smiles.

She looked down at her snowy boots, nervously chewing on one of her red ribbons.

Just then, her mother pulled the soggy ribbon from her mouth as Mia's new teacher arrived. The teacher was short and plump, wearing a bright scarf and a warm smile. She spoke to Mia's mother, but Mia didn't understand the new language. Her mother hugged them tightly and left.

The door closed behind them, leaving Mia feeling lonely and confused.

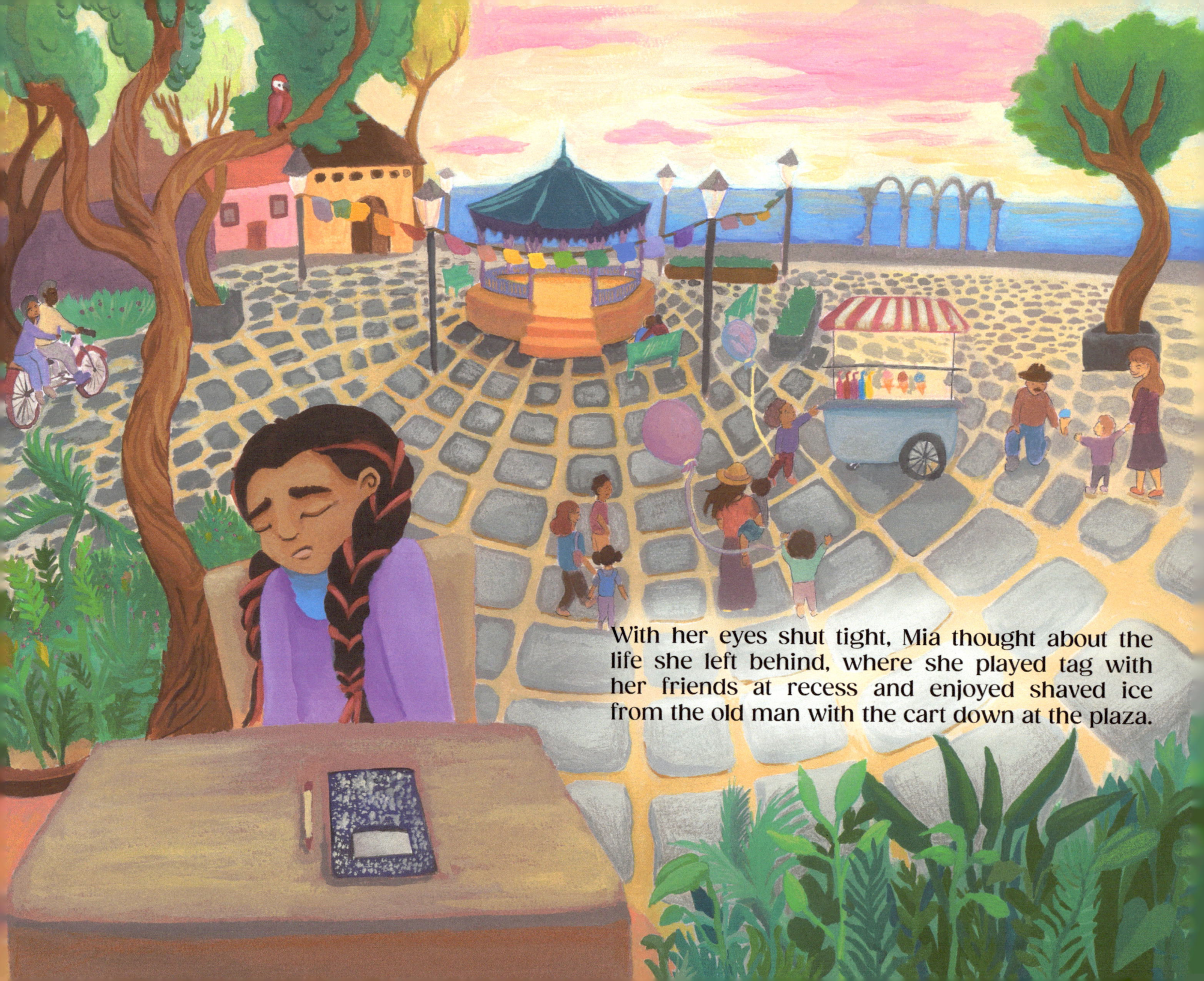

With her eyes shut tight, Mia thought about the life she left behind, where she played tag with her friends at recess and enjoyed shaved ice from the old man with the cart down at the plaza.

Suddenly, Mia noticed a girl standing by her, with long blonde braids. She smiled brightly as she showed Mia her blue ribbons. Mia gave her a shy smile, feeling a little less lonely.

"I can do this!" Mia thought, determined to be strong, just like she promised Abuela the day they left.

But by the end of the day, Mia didn't feel strong. She was tired and frustrated. "I want to go back home to Mexico," she told Marco.

Seeing his sister's unhappy face, Marco pulled her in close. "Try to think of this place as a big adventure. You never know; we might learn to like it here."

As the bus rolled home, Mia leaned into her big brother's arms. "Okay, *hermano*," Mia said, her heart warming a bit. "I will try."

The next day at recess, Mia was alone, kicking at the snow. Suddenly, the girl with the blonde braids reached for her hand and led Mia up a hill. "I'm Tessa," she said in a friendly voice. Mia noticed Tessa was dragging a sled.

"Sit with me!" Tessa said, patting the sled.

Mia gazed blankly at Tessa, unsure of what to say. Just then, Marco appeared out of nowhere, his eyes sparkling with mischief. "*¡Siéntate!*" he encouraged gently.

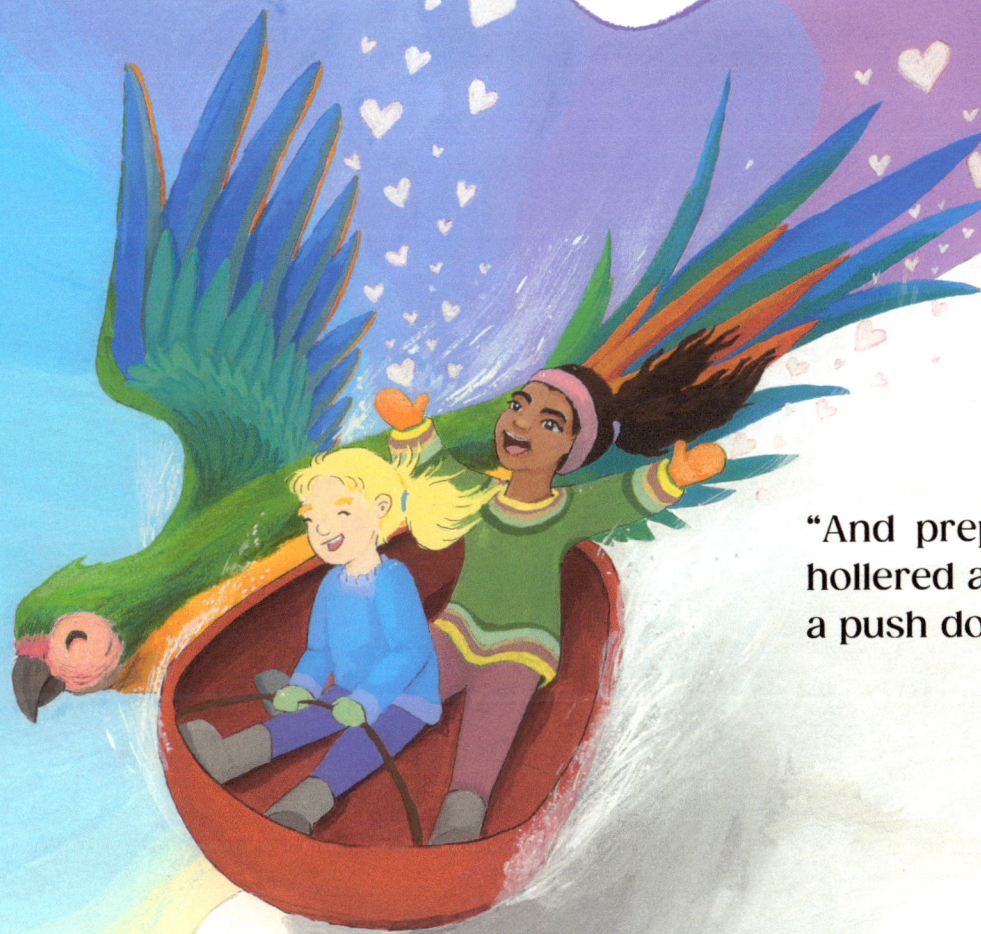

"And prepare to fly!" he hollered as he gave them a push down the hill.

Mia felt a thrill as they zoomed down the hill, Marco cheering behind them. She burst out in laughter and shouts, imagining herself soaring like the parrots that flew over her Abuela's house.

Mia and Tessa gained speed down the hill, hit a bump, and then tumbled over. The girls giggled and brushed the snow from their braids. For a little while, Mia forgot her sadness and felt joy echoing in the cold air. Soon, the school bell rang, and together, they walked back inside, all covered in snow.

Every day that week, Mia and her new friend hurried through lunch to get back to the sledding hill. Secretly, Marco checked in on his little sister, but when he saw that Mia was playing, he went back to making snow forts with the boys his own age.

Many days later, when the sunlight lingered longer in the sky and the air felt warmer, Mia finally got to talk to her grandmother. "Abuela, guess what? I went sledding!" she shared excitedly. As her grandmother listened, Mia told stories from school. She talked about her kind teacher and, of course, Tessa, who didn't care that Mia couldn't speak the same way she did.

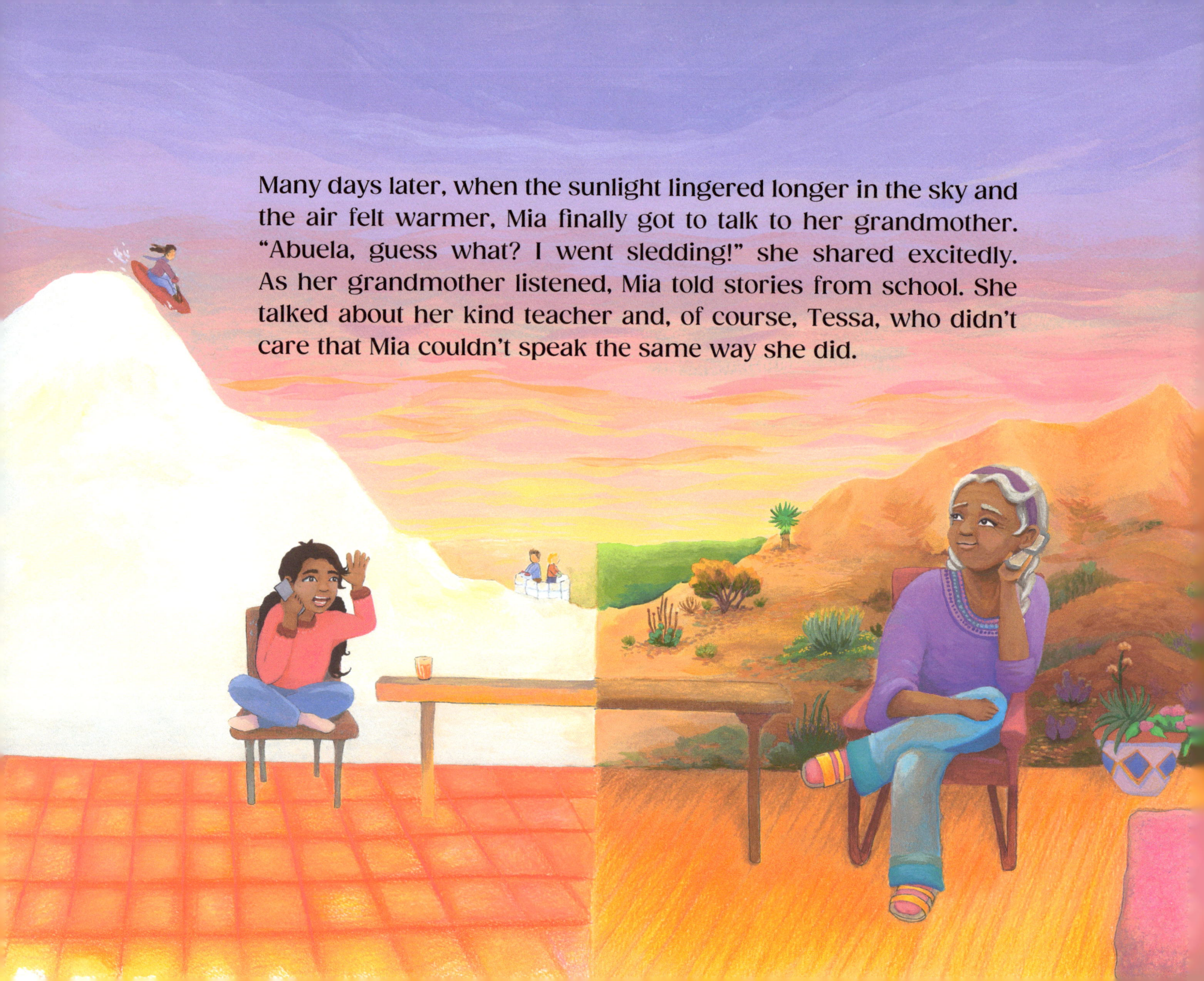

After the call, Mia headed to the kitchen, where she found a glass of freshly squeezed orange juice. She took a sip and noticed it tasted different—sweeter! Just then, she heard the swishing sound of her brother bounding around the apartment in his snow pants.

"Let's go play in the snow!" Marco exclaimed.

"Coming!" Mia replied, tossing her cup in the sink as she ran outside.

In the sunny spot by their apartment building, Mia spotted tiny purple flowers pushing through the snow. She marveled at how something so small could bloom in such cold.

At the sledding hill, Mia realized how far she had come. It had taken just one friend's kindness to help her through the lonely times. Like the tiny flowers, she knew she would thrive here too.

As the sun dipped behind the mountains and the air grew chilly, Mia squeezed Marco's hand. "*Vámonos*, Marco. Let's go home."